POLE DOG

by TRES SEYMOUR

pictures by DAVID SOMAN

ORCHARD BOOKS   NEW YORK

Orchard Books, 95 Madison Avenue, New York, NY 10016

Manufactured in the United States of America. Printed by Barton Press, Inc.
Bound by Horowitz/Rae. Book design by Mina Greenstein.
The text of this book is set in 20 point Meridien Medium. The illustrations are pastels
reproduced in full color.   10 9 8 7 6 5 4 3 2 1

Library of Congress Cataloging-in-Publication Data
Seymour, Tres. Pole Dog / by Tres Seymour ; pictures by David Soman.
p.   cm. "A Richard Jackson book"—P.
Summary: An old dog is left by a telephone pole and waits and
waits for someone to care for him.
ISBN 0-531-05470-5   ISBN 0-531-08620-8 (lib. bdg.)
[1. Dogs—Fiction.   2. Animals—Treatment—Fiction.   3. Stories in rhyme.]
I. Soman, David, ill.   II. Title. PZ8.3.S496Po 1993 [E]—dc20 92-24174

To my mother, who named him

—T.S.

To Avi, Joey, Maia, and Andrew,
always family, with love

—D.S.

Old dog, old dog,
Left by the telephone pole dog.

They're coming back for their old dog.

They're coming back for their old dog.

They're coming back for their old dog.

Won't they come for their old dog?

Old dog, old dog,
Waits by the telephone pole dog.

Pole Dog.

Night fog.
Cold dog.
Waiting by the pole dog.

When will they come for their old dog?

Hungry, hungry Pole Dog.

Eating garbage Pole Dog.

Chasing after Pole Dog.
Shooting guns at Pole Dog.

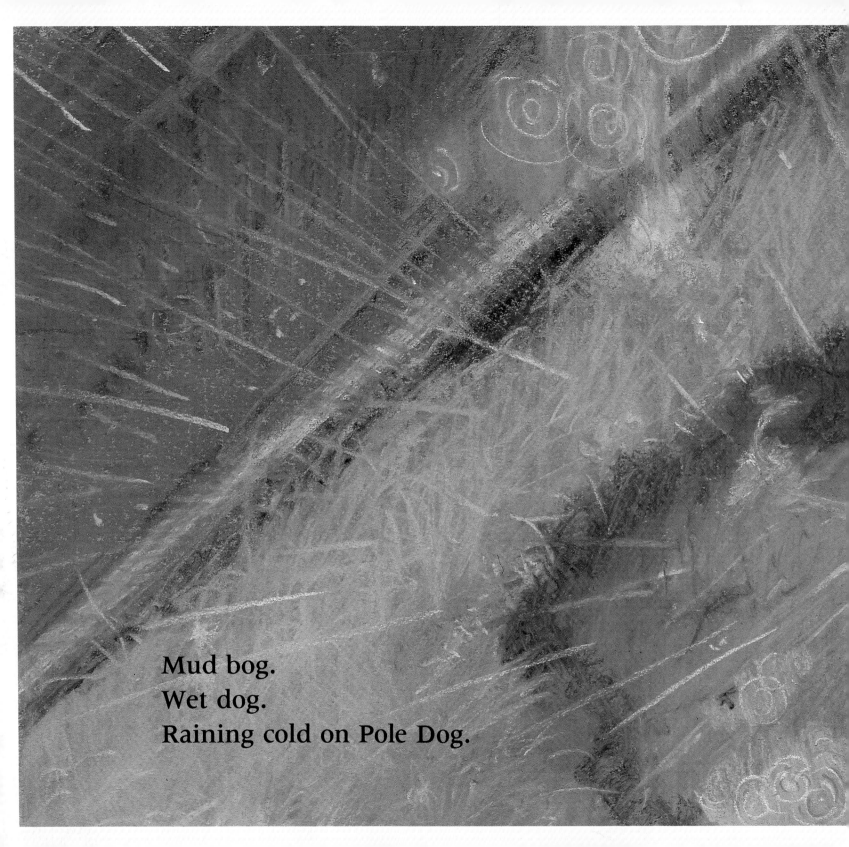

Mud bog.
Wet dog.
Raining cold on Pole Dog.

They won't come for their old dog.

Nobody wants an old dog.

Nobody wants a Pole Dog.

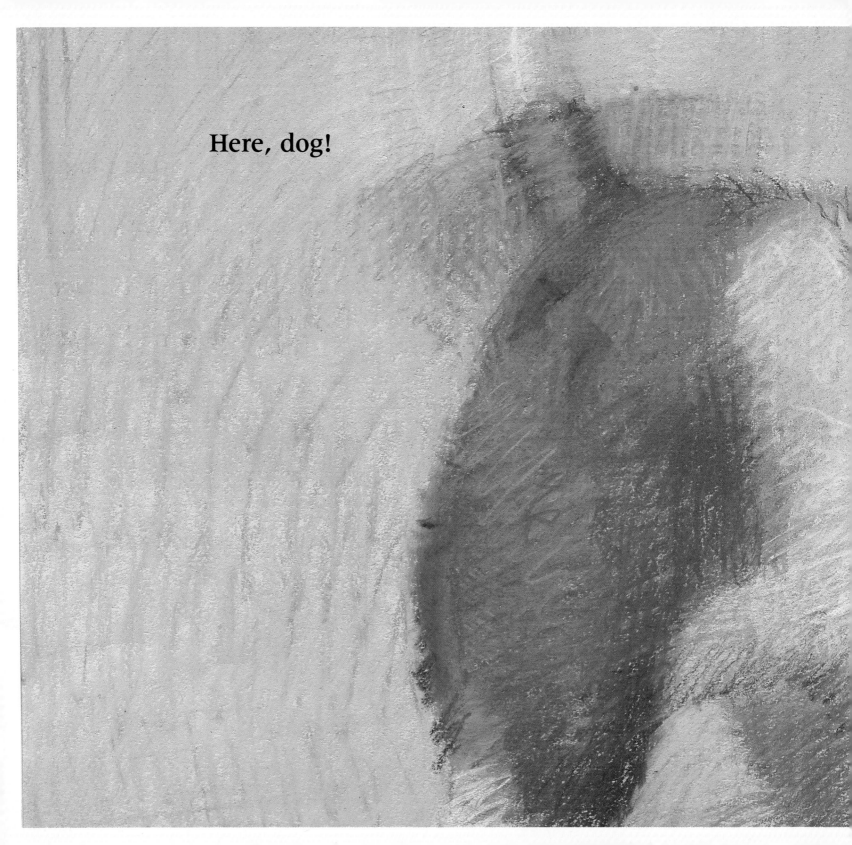

Here, dog!

Call dog?
Somebody wants an old dog!

Hug dog, hold dog.

Good old dog.

Few dogs are as lucky as Pole Dog. Hundreds of dogs and cats are left on the roadside each day by people who don't want them or can't care for them. Some of these people say, "They are better off in the wild, where they can hunt." But they are not. These animals often become sick and hungry, and many die.

If you see a dog or cat that has been abandoned, call the Humane Society or the animal shelter in your area. Their numbers are in the telephone book.